Sleight Of Fate

and various Sherlock Holmes puzzles

By Balaji Narasimhan

Paperback ISBN 978-1-78092-477-9
ePub ISBN 978-1-78092-478-6
PDF ISBN 978-1-78092-479-3

Published in the UK by MX Publishing
335 Princess Park Manor, Royal Drive, London, N11 3GX
www.mxpublishing.com

Cover design by www.staunch.com

"What object is served by this circle of misery and violence and fear? It must tend to some end, or else our universe is ruled by chance, which is unthinkable."

Sherlock Holmes, The Adventure of the Cardboard Box

To Carolyn and Joel Senter, who published my first book and helped me find publishers for my second and third ones

Acknowledgements

The author wishes to thank Satya Vivvek for urging him to write this book; S Suresh Kumar for teaching him the importance of 'vazhkai' ('life' in the Tamizh language); Alistair MacLean for writing Fear is the Key, a great book on revenge; and SR Ramakrishna for reading the first draft and saying that this was worth publishing.

Contents

About the book 1
About the author 2
Prologue 3
Chapter 1 6
Chapter 2 9
Chapter 3 12
Chapter 4 15
Chapter 5 18
Chapter 6 21
Chapter 7 24
Chapter 8 27
Chapter 9 30
Chapter 10 33
Chapter 11 36
Chapter 12 39
Chapter 13 42
Chapter 14 45
Chapter 15 48
Chapter 16 51
Chapter 17 54
Epilogue 57
Author's after word.. 61
Sherlock Holmes and the Bujagotamma Diamond 62
Do we need a "new age" Sherlock Holmes? 71
Happy Birthday Mr Sherlock Holmes! 73
Sherlock's Illusion... 76
Sherlock Holmes and The Nakshatras Of Vesuvius 82
VESUVIUS MAY ERUPT ON 18 MARCH 1944 90

About the book

Most works of fiction that concern torture usually talk about one of two things—they are about a sadist hurting an innocent person or a good guy getting even by inflicting anguish on a cruel character who has harmed him.

The main story in this book looks at a third alternative—what if both the torturer and the victim are merely puppets in the hands of destiny? What if they are actually good people who have been forced by kismet to inflict and absorb pain?

While this is in a way a book about hate, it also looks at how karma—which is usually seen as being cruelly fatalistic—can lead to forgiveness.

The book also contains additional short stories and Sherlock Holmes puzzles.

About the author

Balaji Narasimhan is an IT journalist and columnist with close to two decades of writing experience. His interest in Sherlock Holmes dates back to his teenage years and his first column in 1995, which was written under the nom-de-plume of RoyalE, carried the silhouette of Sherlock Holmes.

His pursuit of subjects as varied as Vedic Astrology and religion can be attributed to his affection towards logic, which he picked up from Sherlock Holmes.

He has previously authored Sherlock Holmes: Solutions from the Sussex Downs, which was published in USA in 2001. He has also edited The Partial Art of Detection, which was published in Japan in 2003. You can follow him on Twitter @sherlockbalaji

Prologue

People think that I should write because I'm creative. I think that this is a bit like telling a curvy blonde that she should become a gangster's moll.

The woman who sat in front me was no moll. She was dignified and wore the most beautiful and sophisticated diamond choker ever made.

I know. Because I made it myself.

Normally, most women wearing costly jewellery like to touch them from time to time to reassure themselves that they are still there. But the lady in front of me couldn't have done this because I had taken the precaution of tying her hands and feet to the chair.

Not that she would have to touch the choker to see if it was still there. It was not going to come off until it killed her.

"Good morning, my lady," I said. It was evening but what the heck, we sat in a windowless room in a basement, so she would never know the time of the day. And I'm not the sort of person who forgets the small courtesies of life just because I'm going to kill somebody.

And I wanted to kill her because I hated her. Anger is like a mutated seed while hate represents toxic water. And from these two, only an ugly tree can bloom.

"Where am I?" She still seemed a little dazed, clearly the Mickey I had slipped into her coffee to fit the choker around her neck had not worn off completely.

"All in good time, my lady. Remember the unique necklace I promised to show you? Well, as you can see from your reflection in the large mirror behind me, it is quite a stunner, isn't it?"

She tried to move and found herself firmly anchored to the chair. "Let me go!" she screamed.

I pressed a small button on the remote in my hand and she choked.

"The choker you are wearing is controlled by this remote. As you can see, it has three buttons. I just pressed the green button, which caused the choker to tighten around your neck for five seconds. If I press the red button, it will choke you for ten seconds."

"What will the blue button do?" she asked. Suddenly she was no longer interested in finding out where she was.

"Ah, the blue button. Trust me, it will not choke."

"You mean, if you press that, it will remove the diamond choker and I will be free to go?"

I laughed and it was not a pleasant sound, at least for her. "If I press that, specially placed blades inside the choker would be activated, severing your jugular veins and carotid arteries."

"You mean, if you press that, I will die?" Fear touched her eyes and her face turned a few shades paler.

"An excellent deduction, my lady. And talking of detectives, I presume that you are familiar with the works of Sherlock Holmes?"

"I have won several quizzes in English literature," she said numbly. I didn't blame her, it is hard to get used to the idea of dying.

"Well, make sure you win this one. In 'A Scandal in Bohemia' Sherlock Holmes says that seventeen steps lead up from the hall to his room. I will therefore ask you seventeen questions. Answer them correctly and I will let you live. If you make one mistake, I will press the green button. For the second mistake, I will press the red button."

I paused for effect and then said, "If you make a third mistake, I will press the blue button."

I opened my laptop, started a computer program that would throw up quiz questions and said, "I hope you win."

Actually, I hoped she would die. But one doesn't tell a nice lady such things to her face.

Chapter 1

The torturer's thoughts

I have always loved perfection.

As a child, I have always got, if not the highest marks, then something close to them.

In a way, though I have never been described as a person who has touched perfection, I have always tried to attain the pinnacle of perfection.

To me, everything has to be just right, and the lady in front of me is a case in point.

I mean, I could easily shot her in the streets, but that would not have been right, right?

That is why I have worked so hard on the necklace she is now wearing. I tested the timers and the motors—tiny but powerful—that controlled the amount of time the choking pressure was applied, and the intensity of the strain.

I have seldom been cruel to anybody—man or animal—but this is something I must do.

You might think that I'm somebody who worked in a concentration camp, but I'm not. I have contributed liberally in the past to orphanages and to animal shelters.

In fact, before today, the only animal that has died by my hands is an old dog to whose neck I fixed the collar to see if pressing the blue button actually caused death.

This dog was on its last legs, but I still wept when my invention worked. You see, if I did kill the lady in front of me, I wanted to do it as painlessly as possible.

That is why I have a revolver in my pocket. If my invention doesn't kill her quickly in the end, I will blow her brains out and provide her with instant oblivion.

Life has not always given me the right chances, but I'm an honest man. I would give her the chance that life never gave me.

The quiz

"'I read nothing except the criminal news and the agony column. The latter is always instructive.' What story is this taken from?" I asked her.

She smiled, which meant that she knew the answer. "The Adventure of the Noble Bachelor," she said.

Good. I don't want her blood on my hands. If she answers all the questions right, it will be my pleasure to release her.

But, some part of me still cries out for revenge...

The victim's thoughts

When one is bound hand and foot to a chair and wearing a necklace that can kill instantly, one doesn't feel like giving self introductions.

But still, permit me. I am the only daughter of a prominent jeweller, long deceased. My dad had two weaknesses—spoiling me silly with the best of gifts and trying to make more and more money. While the former was good, the latter was usually achieved by destroying the dreams of others.

Wealth is as addictive as tobacco, and since society abhors the latter while praising the former, it is even harder to give up.

Though I have always had what I wanted, I think that I may say that I have also been kind to people. My mom told me that when I was a kid, I cried because the cook's son didn't have good toys, and this forced my dad to buy some for him.

After my parents died, I have made a lot of money, but I run a string of orphanages, animal shelters and homes for the old and infirm.

God has given me a lot, and I have spread what He has given me among His children.

So, why am I fighting for my life now?

Chapter 2

The torturer's thoughts

Designing the perfect diamond necklace means more than adding a lot of sparkling diamonds. It means that you have to define, first of all, the meaning of perfection itself.

Many people speak of perfection and quality without understanding these words. To a film director, a perfect plate of glass is a thin one that won't hurt the stunt artist when he drives a bike through it. To a security man, a perfect plate of glass is something that can stop a bullet and protect a VIP standing behind it and delivering a lecture.

To me, a perfect necklace is something that cannot be stolen.

You may want to laugh at me for saying this, but there is nothing funny about getting your necklace stolen while walking on a street, or losing it during a 'power failure' as happens so often in many films.

How does one design something like this? For one thing, the clasp has to be solid so that it cannot be easily removed. And the base metal on which the diamonds are mounted should be sturdy and resist wrenching.

Of course, if somebody were to pull such a necklace really hard, it may literally yank off the neck of the wearer. But since no chain snatcher is going to industriously saw a necklace off a lady's neck right in front of her, chances of this happening are remote.

One thing that has fascinated me is technology. One day, my aim is to create a necklace that comes with its own fingerprint reader, the way mobile phones come with an IMEI number. This way, even if somebody steals the necklace, they can't wear it, though they could possibly break it down and sell the jewels separately.

But this is something that I might work on in the future. Today, the only necklace I'm concerned about is the one adoring the neck of the lady in front of me.

The quiz

"'Chance has put in our way a most singular and whimsical problem, and its solution is its own reward.' Do you know in which story Sherlock Holmes said this?"

The lady smiled again. "The Adventure of the Blue Carbuncle," she said, with relief in her voice.

Good, my lady, but are you good enough? I still have fifteen more questions for you and you have just two chances of getting the answers wrong. After that, the next mistake you make will be the last one ever.

The victim's thoughts

Diamonds have always been my weakness. Even as a child, my mom has told me that I would keep tugging at her necklaces when she lifted me, even wrenching some of them right off her neck by breaking the slender clasp.

I'm sure that mom would have liked a necklace like the one I'm wearing. The diamonds are big and flawless.

Of course, you need money to buy diamonds and money is not just the root of all evil, it also represents the stem and the leaves—in fact, the whole tree itself.

It is therefore no surprise that in the Sherlock Holmes story mentioned above, The Great Detective says that, "In the larger and older jewels every facet may stand for a bloody deed." How much blood has been spilt over the diamonds around my neck? And if I fail thrice—and I'm sure that, as time passes, the questions will get tougher, this much is clear from the grim expression in the eyes of my torturer—will the blades that cut my neck cause these diamonds to be drenched crimson? I shudder at that very thought!

Chapter 3

The torturer's thoughts

I still remember the day I attended the seminar on jewels.

There was the usual stuff, which was interesting, though commonplace. There were stalls where new patterns were shown and experts were talking about how different alloys with gold could give near-cent-percent pure gold ornaments.

Nobody, it seemed, was interested in my unbreakable chain. In a way, this was good, because it showed that I had a revolutionary idea. From another point of view, it was not so ideal because jewellers may be that much more against the idea.

One stall I visited had an interesting idea to woo customers. You filled up a form giving your personal data and the idea for a new design, and if you won, you were supposed to win a gold ring.

My idea, I felt, was too good to be written on such a form. Why not discuss it with the owner of the jewellery store? Fortunately for me, he was right there, so I could take his business card from him. I promised to give him a call soon.

Ad thus began my saga of suffering. Suffering leads to prayer and prayer leads to liberation, but since all my thoughts were aimed at fulfilling my hatred, liberation was not mine to grasp.

The quiz

"'I have satisfied myself that by no exertion of my strength can I transfix the pig with a single blow.' Where did Holmes say this? Do you know?" I asked the lady.

This was a simple question and immediately the lady told me that it appeared in The Adventure of Black Peter.

I agree with you, Mr Holmes. Many pigs take many blows before they succumb. But I'm a patient man.

The victim's thoughts

I hate my torturer. How I wish I could see him hanging on a hook like a pig at a butcher's! He deserves to be shot down like a rabid dog.

You may think that my heart is as hard as the diamonds I love, but this is not true. In fact, diamonds form an integral part of the kindness I have shown to others.

A classic case in point concerned a trip to a famous jeweller's shop in another city. Usually, I get my jewels designed in my own shop, but when I saw a sparkling diamond set at this jeweller's, I just had to own it.

After I bought it—it cost a fortune, but what is money to somebody as rich as me?—I was stepping out when I saw a poor beggar. She was clothed in rags and from the look on her face it was clear that she had not had a decent meal for a while.

I felt a twinge of guilt—was it right that I should enjoy so much, while other around me suffered?

I immediately decided that I should share my wealth with others. I took the lady to a small home for destitute women.

And I didn't stop there. In my own city, I built a large home where thousands of old people who had nobody to call their own could spend their last days on earth with dignity. And the beggar woman was the first person whom I admitted there. She died a few years ago, but before she did, she wrote the most beautiful letter I have ever received from anybody.

I still have this letter with me in my purse. I have laminated it to protect it from the elements and time and again, I gaze upon it. This letter and this first beggar were what have made me a prominent donor in my city today.

Chapter 4

The torturer's thoughts

I called up the jeweller and met him after fixing an appointment with him.

There are some people who have an open and honest face, but this fellow was not one of their ranks. He looked like the sort of person who had pretty poor standards and ethics.

Still, if I was keen on protecting my invention, I was desperate to ensure that my pet project saw the light of day. And since he was showing interest while others weren't, my choices were pretty limited.

But just because I was desperate did not mean that I took no precautions. I was meeting the jeweller in December, but way back in April, I had opened a bank locker and kept the designs of my choker there.

I never operated that particular locker again. In my opinion, this meant that if somebody cheated me and claimed my invention as his own, then I could tell the court that I had thought of the idea of the necklace originally. The records maintained by the bank would show that they had been deposited in my safety locker in April and never operated again.

Of course, if it came to a court case, I may not have the resources to fight a long drawn case. Still, this was one precaution that I could afford to take, and I took it.

But while I was something of a genius when it came to jewels, I was unsophisticated in the ways of the world—and this would one day cost me dearly. But I did not know it that day, when the jeweller told me that he considered my invention an amazing one. He promised me that I would become rich and famous because of my design. And fool that I was, I believed him.

And I suffered. Suffering is ennobling only when it comes with a sense of detachment—otherwise, it can make you selfish and petty, the way it made me.

The quiz

"'He has all the Celtic power of quick intuition, but he is deficient in the wide range of exact knowledge which is essential to the higher developments of his art.' Where did Sherlock Holmes say this?"

I will give the lady one thing—though I had a very poor opinion of her and her family, she knew her literature, especially Sherlock Holmes. Without any hesitation, she told me that this line appeared in The Sign of Four.

Right, my lady. And as long as you stay right, you will stay alive.

The victim's thoughts

My mom and dad were as opposite as they come. Mom was religious and had high morals, but dad felt that his only goal was making money.

Many people like money—I do, because it helps me to buy diamonds and serve the poor—but for dad, money was everything. He even measured his affection for us based upon what he could afford to buy for us.

A very unfortunate thing was that he used to get designs for jewellery made from unsuspecting people. After promising to make them famous, he would cheat them, thereby keeping the money—and the credit for the fine jewellery—all to himself.

Mom tried to do something about it, but since the desire for money and name were almost burnt into dad's DNA, there was not much she could do about it.

Chapter 5

The torturer's thoughts

Now that the jeweller had agreed to make my safety necklace, I decided that it was time to approach the issue of a contract.

He said that he had a better idea—he wanted me to become the director of a special unit that would make the unbreakable necklace.

Regarding the drawing up of the contract, he said that he would have to first check up with a few others, but he said that, from that moment on, I was an employee and offered me a fat salary. In fact, he even offered one month's salary extra right then and there because he said that he was thrilled with my idea.

Looking back, I think that I did a foolish thing. But at that moment, I felt reasonably secure. Any doubts I had were driven away by the wave of elation that swept over me—I was a director, no less, with the full power to bring my dream to fruition and had an admirable salary that would allow me to afford a nice big house and a sleek new car. What more did a man want?

I remember those days of pleasure the way I remember my pain now. Both the psychiatrist and the vindictive man must remember all the mental pain they have personally faced in life—the former so that he never inflicts it upon his patients, and the latter so that he knows exactly what hurts the most and therefore can cause maximum damage to the object of his hatred.

The quiz

"'There is nothing in which deduction is so necessary as in religion. It can be built up as an exact science by the reasoner. Our highest assurance of the goodness of providence seems to me to rest in the flowers. All other things, our powers, our desires, our food, are all really necessary for our existence in the first instance. But this rose is an extra. Its smell and its colour are an embellishment of life, not a condition of it. It is only goodness which gives extras, and so I say again that we have much to hope from the flowers.' Where did Holmes say this?"

"The Naval Treaty," she replied at once.

The victim's thoughts

If only life were as easy as answering the quiz questions that my tormentor is asking me to solve!

But life is seldom easy. Take my mother, for instance. She had everything—several nice houses and cars, an adoring daughter and a loving husband. But still she was worried because she was God fearing and dad's unethical practises made her fear for his soul.

Since her attempts to change him were in vain, she started seeing what documents he stored at home. When she found that he had cheated somebody, she used to secretly make amends. She was very worried that the people whom he cheated would curse him and their ill wishes would lead to our ruin.

But when dad found out about this, he stopped getting documents home. Later, in order to ensure that we never knew about his underhand dealings, he even stopped providing documents to people so that they would have nothing to hold against him in a court of law.

Because of this, there was nothing that mom could find out about his business affairs. And since she could no longer make amends with the people whom dad cheated, she feared that the mountain of his sins would keep growing unchecked.

Chapter 6

The torturer's thoughts

The elation of getting all the things I wanted—a house, car, prestige, and my dream project—was soon replaced by sheer hard work, which alone can sustain an endeavour as important as the one I undertook.

Before I got this job, everything was in the realm of theory. But now, I moved to the experimentation stage. Which base would make the chain unbreakable? What was the best way to place the diamonds? Is there some way in which I can ensure that a thief could never take it apart by melting the metal and selling the diamonds separately?

Some of the plans I had were possible, but some were not. But the only way I could determine this was by actually trying it out and then determining if it was feasible in practice.

Needless to say, there were a lot of false starts, promises that crumbled within a short period of time. But with iron in my heart, I struggled. Countless are the nights when I slept in the office for a few hours and then woke up with the burning desire to continue with my plans.

And finally, I made it. True, it was not perfect—the necklace could be melted and the diamonds could be sold separately—but otherwise it was ideal.

It even came with a tiny battery that powered a fingerprint reader, which alone could open the clasp. This meant that you had to register it before you used it. I wonder why nobody thought about this before—after all, if your e-mail ID comes with basic password security, why not use fingerprint technology for a priceless necklace? True, it made the necklace bigger, but I felt it was worth it.

One could yank it off somebody's neck, but if this happened, a shrill sound would be emitted, which would no doubt aid in apprehending the thief.

But, when I showed the plans and the final piece to the jeweller, he threw me out of the company for embezzlement, though I had not stolen a penny from him.

And so I, who had drunk the nectar of happiness earlier, was forced to drink the poison of sorrow. But I have had so much of the latter recently that I have forgotten what the former tastes like.

The quiz

"'You observed that her right glove was torn at the forefinger, but you did not apparently see that both the glove and finger were stained with violet ink.' Have you any idea where Holmes said this?"

"A Case of Identity," she smiled. "And talking of identity, do you mind telling me your own?"

No lady, I will not tell you. You will go to the grave without knowing anything about me.

The victim's thoughts

I still remember the worst day of my life. It was the day when mom died.

When she died, the only thing she regretted about her life was dad's incorrigible character. She made me promise her on her deathbed that I would always stick to high principles throughout life. I did.

Many years after dad died, I am proud to say that I have made his business grow considerably. But greater pride I take in the fact that I have always honoured the word I gave mom. Secretly, I also feel vindicated because I have turned greater profits than dad by being more honest than him—clear proof that God rewards the virtuous.

But why is this happening to me now? What did I do wrong to deserve this?

Chapter 7

The torturer's thoughts

Sometimes, one feels so numb that one doesn't register pain for a while, but this is only temporary. The anguish soon comes back and hits you really hard. And this is what happened to me when I lost my job and found out that I would get neither royalty nor credit for my invention.

I could have drowned my sorrows in drink, but I did not—for, life is bitter, and why do I need alcohol, which is also bitter?

Thanks to my courage, I did not lose heart. I was right and since justice was with me, so was God. Though I lost the car and the house, which had been registered with the jeweller's company, I had managed to save quite a bit of money from my salary.

Confident that this money would see me through, I approached a lawyer and asked him to file a case against the jeweller.

The lawyer said that he would try his best to help me. When he asked me for proof about how I created the diamond necklace, I told him that, though I had not got it patented, I had the plans locked away in a bank locker. If the court was told to verify the date of last usage of the safety deposit locker at the bank, they would know that the plans had been deposited way before I met the jeweller. This would prove that I had created the concept of my necklace before meeting this jeweller.

My lawyer felt that this was reasonable proof, but said that one could never predict how the courts would consider this matter. Still, he was of the opinion that this was something to go by and promised to file a case against the jeweller at the earliest for defamation and wrongful termination of employment.

I came away from the lawyer's office in a pleasant frame of mind. True, I wanted to have my creation unveiled at a glittering function with a hundred people clapping their hands as my necklace was shown to the world. But if this court case went well, it would generate a lot of publicity in the Press, and I would ultimately benefit from it.

The quiz

"'I don't mind confessing to you that I have always had an idea that I would have made a highly efficient criminal. This is the chance of my lifetime in that direction.' Any idea where Holmes said this?"

"The Adventure of Charles Augustus Milverton," she said. Correct as usual. Will I have to let her go if she answers the remaining ten questions correctly? I'm honour-bound to do this, but how I hate the thought of her getting away scot free! Still, I do have some other tricks up my sleeve...

The victim's thoughts

After mom died, I told dad that though she loved him because of his generosity and kindness, she was most worried about him because of his crooked ways.

Initially, he was keen on changing his evil ways, but unfortunately, he soon reverted to his old path and there was little that I could do to amend him.

But while I respected dad and loved him, ultimately, I was bound to the word I gave mom on her deathbed.

So I decided that I would spend some of dad's ill-gotten wealth on charitable causes. I started in a small way, by donating liberally to animal shelters, homes for the old and infirm, hospitals, temples, and other causes considered noble by society.

I hope that God forgives dad because his money is ultimately being put to good use.

Chapter 8

The torturer's thoughts

If you have never fought a court case before, let me tell you that it is hard even if you do happen to have justice on your side.

This is primarily because a man is presumed innocent until proven guilty. Since it was my problem to prove that the jeweller had stolen the designs for my necklace, I had to show beyond all reasonable doubt that he was a crook. If even a shadow of disbelief persisted, then the courts would be forced to allow him to walk away a free man.

The jeweller had far more resources than me and though my lawyer was a capable man, the opposition had access to more money and therefore more highly paid lawyers.

Also, once the matter entered the courts, I could no longer talk about it and though this also applied to the jeweller, he had his cronies, who sowed seeds of doubt against me. And while the honourable judges are above such things, witnesses and others associated with the case—including the public—are not, and the stories that were being circulated against me were maligning my character.

It was all being done in a subtle way because the jeweller was no doubt afraid that the court would pull him up if anything was said by somebody who was close to him. So he bribed people to hint at moral turpitude in a roundabout way, by making praise sound like criticism.

For instance, one of my old acquaintances from college mentioned to a leading newspaper that he was shocked that a close friend like me—he alluded to the fact that I had allowed him to copy answers from my paper during college exams, which was true—was now himself accused of copying a design. While this could be seen as something in praise of me, it indirectly hinted at the fact that I was capable of bending rules and had some flaws in my character.

The quiz

"'You see, but you do not observe. The distinction is clear.' Where does this like get mentioned?"

"A Scandal in Bohemia."

The victim's thoughts

It is sad to lose one parent, but to lose both is even more painful. The second blow came when dad was diagnosed with cancer. It was one of those rare and incurable ones, and it really broke his spirit.

All along, he had faith in wealth, and now, it let him down. Though treated in the best of hospitals by excellent doctors, he was withering away.

Dad really regretted what was happening to him and felt that all this was happening to him because of the evil way in which he made money. One day, I found him reading the paper and weeping inconsolably. When I asked him why, he pointed to an article that showed how a baby girl abandoned in a dustbin had survived, but a famous businessman had died of a heart attack when surrounded by eminent cardiologists in an ICU. "This is going to be my fate, because fate has betrayed me," he sobbed in anguish.

Oh, daddy! What of all the people you betrayed? I could have asked him this, but this was not the right time. And what use was advice now? Medicine, when taken too late, doesn't cure, but still retains its bitter taste.

Chapter 9

The torturer's thoughts

One of the things that one forgets when one fights a court case is the fact that they can be quite costly and they take a lot of time. One wishes that the courts could function quicker, but justice demands that many procedures should be followed to ensure that the innocent are not punished—and ironically, sometimes, the innocent pay merely because it takes so much time for them to get justice.

Over a period of time, my savings began to dwindle because of my lawyer's fees. My lawyer also hired a senior counsel for certain important court appearances, and his fees were prohibitively expensive.

On top of that, one spends time just running around. You want a certain friend to give you a character testimonial in court, you have to travel to persuade him to come. If you want an expert witness who lives in another city, you have to again travel to meet him, and pay for his travel and boarding when he is in town.

And finally, there are the health problems. The constant tension gets to you and you also end up spending money visiting doctors and taking various medicines to maintain your health in order.

When bad habits ruin you, you can give them up. But what do you do when life itself ruins you?

As the days passed, I turned more and more haggard and when I looked at a mirror, a stranger peered back—a stranger with bloodshot eyes from which all hope was lost, a stranger whose only thoughts dealt with revenge, a stranger whose sole sustaining emotion was hate.

One day, while walking, I saw a new jewellery store being inaugurated. It belonged to my opponent. I saw him get out of a stretch limousine along with the Mayor, who was inaugurating the new store. The jeweller looked really happy, and if I had a gun with me then, I would have shot him dead. God, how I hate that man!

The quiz

"'Does it come within our purview either? Anything is better than stagnation, but really we seem to have been switched on to a Grimms' fairy tale.' Do you know in which story Holmes said this?

"The Adventure of the Sussex Vampire," she said. While she had answered quite a few questions in a second, for this one she paused to think. No doubt she was getting tense, but she had crossed the halfway mark, which meant that the pressure of finishing the quiz in one piece was really weighing her down.

The victim's thoughts

I just finished dad's last rites. I cried bitter tears of sorrow, but one consolation for me was that when he died, he realised the error of his ways. He understood that mom was right all along.

Using this opportunity, I told him that he should start sharing his wealth with others from that very instant. I made him sign a cheque for a large amount and gave it to the hospital so that they could inaugurate a wing for treating poor cancer patients. He died soon after this, and this is, to the best of my knowledge, the first and only time when he has shown kindness while expecting nothing in return.

Chapter 10

The torturer's thoughts

Finally, the case was progressing. My lawyer told the court that the design was mine and to prove it, he said that the plans for the same were locked in my safety deposit locker way back in April last year and that I joined the jeweller's employment only in December of the same year.

My lawyer also gave the keys of the locker to the court. The officials of the court then went to the bank, found that it has not been operated since April, and opened the locker and presented the drawings of the necklace to the court.

It looked like there was some amount of proof to show that I was telling the truth, and this made me feel that I would win. However, the lawyers of the jeweller—I should probably say board of attorneys at law, he had a huge law firm with many top lawyers defending him—came up with a cunning stratagem to defend him.

Apparently, in January last year, robbers had broken into the jeweller's shop and made away with several jewels and papers. The police report at that time, which was drawn up before I put my own designs in the locker, said that various precious stones and designs were stolen.

In a masterpiece of chicanery and mendacity, the opposition lawyers hinted at the fact that the plans for my necklace might have been one of the stolen designs. They did not positively say that I had broken into the jeweller's store and stolen the plans, but since the robbers were never apprehended, they hinted that there was a possibility that I might have got the idea for the unbreakable necklace from there.

"Let's assume, My Lord," said the jeweller's lawyer while concluding his thoughts, "that this gentleman is sitting in a restaurant and the thieves are in the next table discussing the loot. What if their discussion, overheard by the designer here (pointing to me) led to the implantation of the idea of the necklace in the mind of the said designer unconsciously? I'm not saying that this was the way it happened. All I'm saying is that the possibility exists, and this throws a certain amount of doubt and the benefit thereof, My Lord, should be given to my client, the jeweller."

And since there was a remote possibility that the jeweller was innocent, he was released. The court told me to pay damages, but the jeweller graciously said this was not necessary. In fact, it would have been impossible because the court case had ruined me and left me indigent.

The quiz

"'In my profession all sorts of odd knowledge comes useful, and this room of yours is a storehouse of it.' Where did Holmes say this?"

"The Adventure of the Three Garridebs."

The victim's thoughts

Was father solely to blame? Was not society, which has always praised one's capability to earn money, also at fault?

After dad's death, I spent time finding out the full extent of his wealth, and it was enormous. To do what he and my mom wanted, I spent liberally and built several hospitals and temples. I tracked down some of the people whom my dad had cheated and made amends.

I also prayed that God should forgive my dad the sins he had committed. I'm sure that the person tormenting me is somebody whom dad cheated. I have promised to pay him double of what he lost at dad's hands, but he only wants revenge. My suffering as my father's daughter is more important to him than his own personal gain.

Chapter 11

The torturer's thoughts

Just as a lover will think only about his beloved, the ruined man will think only about the person who destroyed him. And after losing everything in the court case—honour, money and, worst of all, hope—all I cared about was killing the jeweller. Forgiveness, they say, is divine, but then again, so is vengeance.

Towards this end, I bought a nice carving knife that was advertised as ideal for cutting pigs (after all, I was going to kill a human pig) and practiced a little by stabbing several pillows in my rage and desire to kill the jeweller.

But there is a vast gap between desire and fulfilment. Even in my own area of expertise, that of designing jewellery, I coveted and my passions were unrequited. And since I have never killed anybody, I was not sure if I would ever have the courage to kill a human being.

But to me, the jeweller had stopped being human when he cheated me. In what way would it have hurt him to have given credit and money to me? After all, it was my idea, wasn't it?

Greed, as several religious scriptures say, tends to lower a man to the level of a beast, and to me the jeweller was somebody who had to be killed like a mad dog.

He had the habit of taking a walk early in the morning and I too started roaming in the same area so that I would know the roads and be capable of making a quick getaway after killing him.

Finally, after planning for a month, I could stand the tension no longer. On a misty morning, I stood at a crossroad and saw him turn a corner ahead of me and walk in my direction. Since it was cold, I had wrapped a blanket around myself and this gave me a better opportunity to hold the knife next to me without being detected.

As the jeweller came nearer, I stabbed him with all the hatred I could muster, but I'm no killer. He lived and told the police about my attempt to kill him. I was apprehended and the judge, after reviewing the case and the previous one concerning my necklace, gave me ten years in prison for attempting the cold blooded murder. He said that the only reason why I was not executed was because the jeweller lived.

The quiz

"'Stand with me here upon the terrace, for it may be the last quiet talk that we shall ever have.' Do you know in which story this quote was mentioned?"

"His Last Bow," she said.

The victim's thoughts

As part of the cleanup, after my dad died, I made my jewellery shop a byword for honesty. The salaries of the staff was raised to ensure that they would be more loyal and have fewer reasons to do anything wrong. I also took great pains to ensure that only gold and precious stones of the highest quality were used in my shop.

Over a period of time, thanks to word-of-mouth publicity, business really boomed. If only dad had done something like this! He would have earned both wealth and respect. Again, if mom had seen me prosper thus, she would have been so proud of me. But fate doesn't grant all desires, and I'm happy that I am making money, helping the poor, and being honest.

And now, all I want to do is get out of this mess in one piece. And somehow, I have a feeling that this is one desire that will not be granted.

Chapter 12

The torturer's thoughts

Jail is terrible. It kills the creative spirit.

The public prosecutor wanted to sentence me to death, but since the Supreme Court has said that death penalty is only possible in the rarest of rare cases, the Judge was reluctant to sentence me to death by hanging, especially since this was my first crime.

But since the prosecution wanted to sentence me to harsh punishment, I was given ten years of rigorous imprisonment, and this meant breaking rocks at the quarry. My hands, which are delicate like those of most artists, have usually held nothing other than the small hammer that we use to beat gold. But now, I am holding a hammer that is really big and breaking stones in the hot sun. I'm literally living by the sweat of my brows.

There was some hope that I would have been able to give up my hate before I entered jail, but now, even that is lost. Every suffering just enhances the hatred that I feel for the jeweller. I feel no remorse for having tried to kill him earlier. Given an opportunity, I would have killed him a thousand times over.

Sometimes, I feel like committing suicide, but we are carefully watched to ensure that we don't take our own lives and embarrass the prison security staff. We use plastic knives and forks like in the airlines, and I have to say that the food is better than what they serve on most planes thanks to the human rights commission keeping a close eye on how we inmates are treated.

But though I want to die almost more than anything else in the world, I want to have my revenge. And it is only this hate that keeps me alive, nothing else. Just as a drunkard drinks because he can't imagine life without alcohol, I stuck to hate because there was no other life for me.

The quiz

"'That is the man who is after me to-night, Watson, and that is the man who is quite unaware that we are after him.' Where does Holmes say this?"

"The Adventure of the Empty House," she said.

Just five more questions to go. Will she make it?

The victim's thoughts

Though I did a lot of good work, I realised that there was one specific thing that I had to do—hold an open competition for new designs.

Dad held a lot of them, but usually used them to cheat people. I have no doubt that the person torturing me is one of those. He might even be the one who tried to murder dad—I'm not sure, I can't recollect the face they printed in the papers many years ago, and in any case, prison can change the way you look. And additionally, many people have tried to kill dad because they have all hated him so much.

I organised several competitions to show that dad's shop had been completely reformed and also to depict that today there was not even a shadow of doubt about our affairs. Eminent judges awarded medals and I created a fund in dad's name to give money to deserving artists. If I used any of their works in any of my jewellery, I always gave them credit and also paid them liberally.

I have done all I can, but the fact that I'm tied to this chair with a diamond choker around my neck that is capable of killing me is clear proof that what I have done has not been enough.

Chapter 13

The torturer's thoughts

After many days in jail, I got some good news, some bad news, and some terrible news.

The good news was that the jeweller died. At last, my enemy was dead, and I could rejoice.

The bad news was that the jeweller died. This meant that I would not be able to have revenge.

But before I could make up my mind about it, I heard that my mom had died.

While discussing the object of my hatred, the jeweller, I have, I fear, completely ignored mentioning my mom. Though I was able to take good care of her earlier, when I became bankrupt and was tossed into jail, she had nowhere to go—I even had to sell the house that I owned to pay the lawyer's fees.

But God is great, and I heard that there was a home for the elderly, where my mom was able to lead a life, if not of happiness, at least one that involved a considerable amount of comfort and dignity. These people were so nice that they even arranged for my mom's last rites and even got permission for me to attend my mom's cremation.

One of my dreams in jail was to once again build my fortunes and ensure that my mother lived in comfort and now, this was no longer possible. The greatest pain in life comes not from humiliation, but from the hope that never translates into reality.

I thought of these folks, who cheerfully looked after old people who had done them no good, and contrasted them with the dead jeweller, who had no compunctions about robbing people like me, people who had worked hard for him. How strange life is!

After the last rites were over, I asked the people running the home for the elderly if I could meet some of the trustees and thank them personally. This was not possible because the main sponsor was constantly travelling, but they promised to tell her that I was touched by their gesture.

I would have really liked to meet the chief patron of this home for the elderly, but even if this is not possible, I pray that such people should prosper. May their tribe increase!

The quiz

"'None of those which come to me are. I am the last court of appeal.' Where did Holmes say this?"

"The Five Orange Pips," she said. As she got closer to the end of the quiz, the lady's face showed increased fear and relief in equal measure. But she was still in danger and she knew it—there were four more questions to go, and three slips meant death.

The victim's thoughts

43

I initially started the competitions to make up for the mistakes my dad had made, but there were several unexpected bonuses as a result of the same. The coverage these competitions got in the Press meant that more customers came to me, and since I won praise from critics and artists alike, my jewellery shop got a lot of respect. Customers all over the city realised that you got extremely good designs in my shop, and even people from other countries started ordering my jewels over the Internet.

Only four more questions. I have promised myself that if I live and my tormentor, true to his word, releases me, I will not go to the police. I will find out how my dad cheated him and then I will make amends. Of course, all this is provided I live!

Chapter 14

The torturer's thoughts

You can only appreciate freedom if you go to jail and then come out again.

Things that people take for granted—the warm sunshine on your face on a cold wintry morning, the sound of birds chirping in the trees, even the mundane cries of the vegetable vendor as he sells his wares—all these take on a new and special significance.

Of course, nobody wants to hire a jailbird, but this didn't deter me. I had a few old contacts who still respected me. With their help, I started a small jewellery store. Since I wanted to be extremely focused, I chose to make only special bridal collections, which were one-of-a-kind. The main guarantee I gave was that, while there would always be variations of a theme, each set would be unique—and they were.

I soon made a decent amount of money. People tend to really spend on jewels when they are getting married, and even in these days, when divorces are so rampant, people still perceive that they are getting married just once in their life and so they spare no expenses. I have known people to borrow heavily in order to finance their daughters' weddings, and since one of the costlier things they invest in is gold and jewellery, I made a tidy packet.

But no matter what I achieved, revenge was something that I thought about every day. Even though the jeweller was dead, I could not forgive him. Forgiveness is a sign of strength only when your enemy seeks it with humility. Only a coward forgives unasked. The jeweller had cheated me by dying before I could get my hands around his neck, but I have tried to locate his family members to see if I can make somebody there pay. I have heard that he has a daughter, who is continuing the family business. One of these days, I tell myself, I will get even. But not right now—I still have to make money. Once I do, I will use that money to get my revenge.

The quiz

"'The ways of fate are indeed hard to understand. If there is not some compensation hereafter, then the world is a cruel jest.' In which story does Holmes say this?"

"The Adventure of the Veiled Lodger."

The victim's thoughts

I don't know what I should feel—fear or relief. I have answered fourteen questions without making a single mistake, and only three more questions remain.

The closer I get to victory, the greater becomes both my hope and my fear. Will I make it to the end? Will I live to see the sun rise again? One appreciates life that much more when one is close to death.

Somehow, I have this fear that my tormentor is playing with me. Maybe, he wanted all along to ask fourteen simple questions, followed three hard ones that would kill me. Who knows?

But I trust in God and one thing that gives me hope is that I can still make two mistakes among the three remaining questions. As long as I get at least one of the answers right, I can still live.

And considering the impeccable record that I hold so far, I'm quite sure that I will finish this quiz with no mistakes, or, at worst, two, and this will still ensure that I live.

I am so happy!

Chapter 15

The torturer's thoughts

As my bank balance again grew to respectable levels, my thoughts turned once again to revenge.

You might think that I had stopped thinking about getting even for a while, but this is not true. Images of the now-dead jeweller continued to haunt me in my nightmares and quite often I would wake up in a cold sweat in the middle of the night. I knew that the only way I could get any peace was by killing the jeweller's daughter. Nothing else would do.

Hate, like citric acid, burns you slowly, but giving up hate means that you have to come face to face with the humiliation that prompted it in the first place—and this is as corrosive as sulphuric acid.

I wanted to have revenge in a unique manner, and so I created a diamond choker that could be used to kill. My pre-prison knowledge of electricity and motors, which I honed to perfection while I was in jail, came in handy now and I created a device that could be used to either stun or kill the victim. I have tested it and I'm confident that it will work when I put it around her neck.

Now, all I had to do was get her to wear it...

The quiz

"Who was the tailor to Jonas Oldacre in The Adventure of the Norwood Builder?"

She paused a moment as if unsteady and then softly said, "I don't know."

"It was Hyams. Now that you have got one answer wrong, I am forced to press the green button, which will choke your neck for five seconds. Please hold your breath if you want."

The victim's thoughts

I knew it! He wanted me to get answers right in the beginning, preferring to taunt and torture me towards the very end.

The green button didn't cause much discomfort. Being choked for five seconds is not at all dangerous, and apart from the annoyance, I don't think that there is anything worth complaining about. And in any case, this was the second time he was using it on me, so I knew how it would feel.

But I was getting more attuned to the way my tormentor was thinking. Though I had no doubt that the next two questions were bound, like this one, to be comparatively tougher than the ones I had answered before, I felt that all I had to do was get one answer right to live.

It is ironic how the mind works. At the beginning, when I had fifteen questions and could only make two mistakes, I thought I could pull it off. Now, with just two questions and the possibility of getting only one wrong, I was faltering.

Well, let's see how the next question goes. I hope that I get it right; it will mean that the last question is largely unnecessary. And if I do end up getting it wrong, I should again remember to hold my breath so that I don't pass out.

I don't think that choking for ten seconds can make you unconscious, but such was the tension I was facing that I thought that anything was possible.

Of course, if I ended up getting the next question and the one after that wrong, then there was nothing that could save me. I just pray that if I get both the remaining questions wrong, at least death should be quick and painless.

Chapter 16

The torturer's thoughts

People have told me that I should give up hate. Actually, one can easily give it up if one has the opportunity to move on. And here, fate plays a key role—if she doesn't allow you to progress, then all you have is your hate to keep you company. And this was what happened to me.

But back to the story. I was finally able to put my plan into action when I attended a function where I knew the jeweller's daughter would also be present. I took great pains to ensure that nobody suspected that I was seeking her out. It was well known that her father had ruined me and if anything happened to her, I would be one of the usual suspects.

But her dad had destroyed so many people that the police would have to end up questioning hundreds of people if anything happened to her and I would just be one of them.

While attending the party, I casually approached her and told her that I had a design on which I wanted her opinion.

"Why don't you participate in one of our competitions?" she asked.

"Well, I'm not sure if it will win. I first want to show it to you so that you can give me your honest feedback.

After that, you can either make the designs yourself, or I can enter it in your competition if you still insist after seeing the design."

"Ok," she conceded.

I got her mobile phone number and promised to call her soon. I did not fix any prior appointment through her secretary because I did not want any entry in any appointment diary that would cause the police to suspect me.

One day I called her and told her that I had to travel abroad suddenly for a few months, so could she come and see the design today itself? I even offered to pick her up in five minutes—I did not want her car parked anywhere near my place. She graciously agreed to take what might be her last trip on earth.

"My, this is the middle of nowhere!" she exclaimed when we finally reached my secret hideout, which I had rented under a different name while wearing a disguise.

"Well, I don't like to work on my secret project in my usual shop. Don't want anybody to steal my designs, you know," I offered by way of explanation.

I took her to the basement and offered her a coffee with a Mickey in it. She soon fainted and when she woke, she wore the diamond choker and was firmly tied to a large chair.

The quiz

"'What the deuce is it to me? You say that we go round the sun. If we went round the moon it would not make a pennyworth of difference to me or my work.' Where did Holmes say this?"

"A Study in Scarlet," she said.

The victim's thoughts

I couldn't believe my ears. This was one of the simplest questions in the entire Sherlock Holmes series. Even children know about this famous quote made by The Great Detective.

I am elated. Even if I get the last question wrong, I will only get choked for ten seconds. There is no way I am going to die today, and the fact that I will once again go on with life makes me feel so warm and pleased.

Chapter 17

One can inflict pain by burning somebody's skin with cigarette butts, breaking bones, poring hot oil over somebody, or by pulling nails.

Or, one can use sheer mental torture and—without laying a finger on one's enemy—make him rue the day he was born.

The latter option is better because after all, while pain belongs to the body, fear belongs to the mind.

And the best way to inflict fear is to move the mind from hopelessness to hope and then back and forth, until the person no longer knows what is happening. He thinks that he is winning when life is going against him and despairs when everything is fine. He fears the light and adores the darkness because he can't tell black from white.

And this is what I have done with my victim. When she first came in, I filled her with despair because she had no idea if she could complete the quiz, while in fact the initial questions were simple. Just as she got her hopes up, I asked her a question that again pushed her back into the pit of fear and despair.

And then, while all hope seemed lost, I asked another easy question. Now, she thinks that she will win.

In fact she even told me, "Since I cannot die now, if you must, you can refrain from asking the last question.

Assume that I'm wrong, press the red button and choke me for ten seconds, and let me live as you promised. Once your desire for revenge is satisfied, please tell me how my father wronged you, and I will try my best to make sure that justice is done to you."

Was she taunting me or was she just being nice? No matter. Having taken the one-way road of revenge, there is no turning back. What is the guarantee that she would not get me thrown behind bars again? And this time, who knows, I may get the death sentence in court, or I may be locked away in jail until I die.

Therefore, I ignored her and asked my last question. "In one of Holmes' most famous stories, a butterfly and a colonel connected with the Nonpareil Club are mentioned. Tell me both their names. If you can only answer one, then you will be choked for ten seconds. If you miss both, then you would have made three mistakes in total, and this means death. The name of the story is not important."

She stared at me shocked. "But you promised me that I only have to answer seventeen questions. Is it right for you to ask an eighteenth one?"

"I promised seventeen questions and I am sticking to my word, which is something that one could never say of your father. However, I never promised that each question would consist of just one part. The seventeenth question actually consists of two parts. Answer both to live."

She lowered her eyes because she didn't know either answer. She had lost in the end, just as I wanted her to lose. If she had lost initially, my revenge would not have been complete. Revenge is not a dish to be served cold. It is a cocktail that has to be served with a twist.

"The answers are Cyclopides and Upwood and they are both mentioned in The Hound of the Baskervilles," I said as I pressed the red button and choked her for twenty seconds. She did not lose consciousness, but gasped for breath when the motors—which were tightening the band around her neck underneath the diamond choker—turned off after the stipulated time frame of ten seconds (sorry if I'm speaking like a lawyer, but I have spent quite some time with them and picked up their language).

"Now," I said, my finger moving towards the blue button, "prepare to die."

Epilogue

"Do you have any last requests before you die?" I asked her.

"I want to live," she said. I thought that she would beg for her life, but she said this with subdued dignity.

"Everybody wants to live," I pointed out.

"Yes. But most only want to live for themselves. I live for myself and others too. I have spent a huge fortune on the underprivileged. If you kill me now, who will look after them? All my wealth will go to some distant relatives, who may just keep it for themselves."

Before I could say anything, she continued, "How will it profit you to kill me? Don't you think that it is better for you to take some money from me and let me live? This way, I can live, you can prosper, and the poor people whom I look after can also benefit. Isn't this logical? Since you have asked me so many Sherlock Holmes quiz questions, tell me, is this not something that Holmes himself would approve of as being the right thing?"

There was much to what she said and I would have listened to her under normal circumstances. But I was blinded by my hate and could not see anything but revenge. Love, they say, is blind, but hate is blinder still. While love only blinds you to the faults of the beloved, hate blinds you to everything, even to the goodness in yourself.

"You are right, my lady," I said, "but since I have thought of nothing but revenge for many years now, I can't think about anything else now."

"You, sir, have quoted Holmes to me many times. Let me also have the same honour. In The Adventure of the Cardboard Box, Sherlock Holmes says, 'What is the meaning of it, Watson? What object is served by this circle of misery and violence and fear? It must tend to some end, or else our universe is ruled by chance, which is unthinkable. But what end? There is the great standing perennial problem to which human reason is as far from an answer as ever'. Tell me, what will your hate fetch you?"

For a second, I almost relented, but my hatred for her father gripped me again and steeled my heart. "It is no use, my lady," I said roughly, "Tell me if you have any last wish, or let me press the blue button and kill you. It is your destiny to die today, so don't fight it."

"Ok," she said, resigned now to her demise. "I want to read a letter by somebody who set me on this route. You will find it in my bag. Please read it to me before you kill me—I can't do it myself because my hands are tied."

Was she trying to make me read a sugary letter from one of the people she had helped in the hope that it would melt my heart? If this was so, she was mistaken, for my heart was like stone. Nothing could save her now.

I opened her bag and read the letter. And then, instead of reading it aloud to her and then pressing the blue button to kill her, I went over to her, dropped the letter in her lap, slit the ropes around her hands, and then gently removed the diamond choker from her neck.

"You can leave," I said.

"What changed your mind?" she asked. "Is this letter from somebody you know?"

"No," I said, "But somebody just like you had helped my mother when I was in jail. I had always wanted to meet the person who helped her, but I could not do it because when I came out of jail, I found out that she was dead. I'm sure that, since you have helped so many people, there are several who want to meet you and thank you personally. I do not want to deprive them this privileged by killing you."

What made me suddenly give up my hate and free her? I don't know and I can't even explain it to myself. It is not as if I have lost my hate for the jeweller—such things happen only in romantic novels. If he was alive today, I would surely kill him a thousand times over.

But I have realised that it is not right to make his daughter pay and therefore I released her. At least, this is what I tell myself, because I don't know for sure exactly why I let her go.

Maybe this is the right answer. And then again, maybe destiny wanted to spare me the sin of killing a good soul, and also perhaps wanted to ensure that the good work she was doing for the poorer sections of society should continue uninterrupted.

And if the latter explanation is true, then she was probably saved not because I changed my mind, but by a sleight of fate.

Author's after word

It's a good thing I have not written a foreword—if I had, I would probably have written about how I wrote this story and that would have become a story in itself.

This was actually a book of hate, where the torturer killed his victim. (In fact, it is for this reason why the jeweller, the torturer and the victim have no names—since the main theme is about hate, these are mere puppets in the story line and why waste time naming puppets?) The letter in her bag was actually supposed to have been written by the torturer's mother. After reading this letter, the torturer regrets killing his victim and then commits suicide.

But I suddenly changed my mind and decided to alter the story's ending in order to make it more positive. I also felt that the idea of the woman having helped the man's mom was too reminiscent of a film story, something which happens in fiction but not in reality, so I changed that too.

The original ending had been planned several months ago, just as the torturer himself had laid the plans to murder the lady. The title of this book at that time was 'Diamond choker drenched crimson'. At the last moment, I decided to change my plans, and this meant that the torturer too had to change his. And since a 'sleight of fate' caused me to alter my plans, I decided that this should be the name of my book. Quite ironic, right? A sleight of fate decided that my book should be called sleight of fate!

Balaji Narasimhan
Bangalore

Sherlock Holmes and the Bujagotamma Diamond

"So, Watson, what do you know of the Bujagotamma diamond?"

I considered the question at length before answering.

"It belonged to Lord Ranganatha of Srirangam, a temple town close to Trichy, from which the famous Trichinopoly cigars come. It was one of the diamonds in His crown. It has the impression of a snake on it, which gave it its name."

"Really?" asked Holmes.

"Yes." I understandably felt smug. After all, it is not every day that I could show off my knowledge to Holmes.

"Pray, continue," said Holmes with a mischievous glint in his eye. He looked tired--he was out on a case and said that he had returned only around 3 AM--but as always, he had shaved before breakfast.

"Bujagotamma is one of the thousand names of Lord Vishnu, one of the Trinity of Hindu Gods. It means one who rules those without limbs and refers to snakes. Vishnu reclines on Adi Sesha, the snake with a thousand hoods. This is one of the reasons why he has this name. Ranganatha is one of the forms of Vishnu."

"Really, Watson, I think that we no longer need to keep the Hindu encyclopaedia. You know the subject so well!"

62

I couldn't tell if Holmes was joking, so I ignored the comment and continued.

"Since India is a part of the British Empire, this stone was forcibly taken from the temple. It is now being displayed at the London Museum. The diamond will soon be set in a crown that will be worn by the Queen."

Holmes looked displeased.

"What is worn by the Gods should remain with Them, Watson."

I was amazed that Holmes was taking such a stance.

"Surely, Holmes, don't tell me that you have started believing in the false Gods of the Hindus?"

"Watson, just as we feel that our God is dear to us, we should also respect the fact that other races too are fond of their Gods."

"And in any case," continued Holmes before I could interrupt him, "we have no right to take costly gems away from the Hindus under the specious garb of disbelief in their religion."

"Well, be it as it may, we now own the diamond. I want to request you to stroll with me to the London Museum later today so that we can have a look at the diamond."

"Well, actually..."

"No ifs or buts, Holmes," I said rather severely. "We are going there today, and that is that."

Before Holmes could reply, the door burst open and a rather overweight gentleman staggered in, followed by Inspector Lestrade.

"I'm ruined!" gasped the fat man before collapsing on the sofa. Holmes and I leapt to our feet and I reached for the brandy bottle and poured him a generous helping. A quick swig bought some colour to his cheeks.

"What's the matter, Lestrade?" asked Holmes, knowing that the inspector would supply the details of the case far quicker than the other man, who was still recovering his breath.

"This is Lord Dixon, who heads the London Museum. Yesterday night, the Bujagotamma diamond was stolen and since then, this man has been mad with grief. That is why I brought him here."

Holmes sat in his favourite chair, relit his pipe and asked, "Any suspects?"

"There are two guards, Mr Holmes," said Lord Dixon, who had regained his breath and wits somewhat. "Fraser and Hayward. Highly dependable men. They have both been with the museum for over twenty years."

"Let's go to the museum. I want to question them," said Holmes.

Lestrade hailed a Hansom and we were soon driving towards the Museum. On the way, Holmes insisted on stopping at No. 3 Pinchin Lane, down near the water's edge at Lambeth to meet Sherman and pick up Toby, the dog who had helped us in The Sign of Four.

We took Toby and went to the museum. Both the guards, Fraser and Hayward, looked at us apprehensively. They knew

64

that if the diamond was not found soon, news of its disappearance would spread quickly and become a blot on their escutcheons."Here, boy," Holmes told Toby and as the dog approached, Holmes lifted it and held it so that it could sniff at the case that had held the Bujagotamma diamond.

Toby took a few eager sniffs and yelped in excitement.

"Good boy. Now, find the thief," said Holmes, putting Toby down.

Toby, instead of dashing off in pursuit of the thief, did something funny. He started sniffing at Holmes.

"He seems to think that you are the thief, Holmes," laughed Lestrade.

"Very funny, Lestrade. I prefer to believe that Toby is more interested in showing his affection for me rather than in catching the thief."

"What should we do?" moaned Lord Dixon, wringing his hands in agony.

Holmes smiled. "Since I seem to be a source of distraction for Toby, I would recommend that Watson and Lestrade should take him outside. The rest of us can wait here."

We did what Holmes suggested. While walking around the building, Toby gave a yelp of delight and rushed towards the compound wall. The ground showed no footprints, but we found something better.

The missing Bujagotamma diamond was lying in a corner hidden under a few small potted plants placed near the compound wall to add a bit of greenery to the otherwise forbidding exterior of the museum.

"Great! We have solved the case!" exclaimed Lestrade.

"Well, we didn't do anything. All the credit has to go to Toby here," I pointed out.

Lestrade gave me a sour look. "True, Toby found the gem. But you need an astute mind like Holmes' or mine to decipher what has happened."

"So, what do your deductions tell you?" I asked.

"Elementary, my dear Watson," said Lestrade. "The thief left by clambering over the wall. While doing so, the diamond evidently fell from his pocket."

"But we still need to solve many things. Who was the thief? How did he get in?"

"Who cares?" countered Lestrade. "We have recovered the diamond. Now, let's get back to the others."

The moment we entered the room, Lestrade took centre stage. Often, he had been forced to stumble along while Holmes' genius solved the case.

But now, with the Bujagotamma diamond firmly in his grasp, he discussed his theory of how the thief had dropped the diamond and how he,

Lestrade, driven by his usual intelligence, sagacity and shrewdness had saved the day.

The only thing that irked Lestrade was the fact that his glory would never become public--this would cause the establishment to lose face. But Lord

Dixon said that he had friends in high places and would ensure that Lestrade would be warmly regarded and even perhaps promoted for his contributions to the Empire.

If Holmes was upset by the fact that he had played no part in the whole episode, he didn't show it. He was quite cheerful when we returned to our rooms in Baker Street.

The next day, as expected, there was no mention of the gem in the papers. Evidently, the powers that be would have felt that it was not appropriate to discuss the issue, especially since certain sections of the media were criticising the Empire for being too free in taking precious and ancient art objects from other countries.

That day, shortly after breakfast, we had a visitor from India. He wore religious marks over his forehead--what they call a 'naamam' in India—and he greeted Holmes with a traditional Indian 'namaste' by pressing the palms of his hands in front of his chest. Holmes greeted him in similar fashion and introduced him to me as Srinivasan Singaperumal, a priest from Srirangam.

"I came the moment I got your telegram. You have it, Mr Holmes?" Singaperumal spoke with a marked accent, but his English was flawless.

Without a word, Holmes handed over a small package to Singaperumal, who accepted it reverentially.

He opened it and revealed a sparkling diamond. I have personally seen diamonds that are larger and brighter, but this particular stone had a small snake-like image embedded in the centre, which made it unique.

"Thank you, Mr Holmes. You have helped to restore the Bujagotamma diamond to its rightful owner, Lord Ranganatha of Srirangam."

"But Holmes! I don't understand! If this is the Bujagotamma diamond, what was the gem that Lestrade found yesterday? And how did this stone come in your possession?" I asked, confused.

Holmes laughed. "My dear Watson, some time back Mr Singaperumal approached me and requested me to help him. He said that for centuries,

the Bujagotamma diamond was worn by Ranganatha. He said that it was wrong to take this gem away from Lord Ranganatha and asked me to help him get it back. That is why I broke into the museum to steal the Bujagotamma diamond."

"So, the gem that Lestrade found was fake?""Yes. Singaperumal said that his spies got word of the plan to forcibly take this diamond from them many months ago. When he told me about it then--we have known each other for many years--I told him to create a replica of it. Singaperumal gave this to me a few days ago and I dropped it near the compound wall, where Lestrade found it."

"But if you had a replica, why didn't you hide the original in India while the British tried to take it away from you?"

"Because, Dr Watson, we feared that if the British detected the forgery then, they would redouble their efforts to find the original. And once they found out, we would have been helpless. No, the best strategy for us was to let them steal the original, and then have somebody like Mr Holmes switch it for us," said Singaperumal.

"Then why create the furore? Holmes could have swapped the stone quietly when he broke into the museum and nobody need have known," I pointed out.

Holmes laughed. "Even now, Watson, nobody knows. If Lestrade had any deductive powers, he would have surmised that the reason why Toby was jumping all over me was because he had detected that I was the thief. We did all this so that we could involve the authorities. If I had swapped the stone silently and somebody had detected the swap at a later date, a hue and cry would have been raised. But now, since Lord Dixon and

Lestrade are indirectly involved, you can be sure that if any suspicions are ever raised, they will try to bury them to protect their own reputations." "But Holmes! Haven't you, by stealing the diamond become an enemy of the Crown?"

Holmes seemed irritated by this question.

"Watson, I have been reading a lot of books on Hinduism that Singaperumal has gifted me. These books have bestowed upon me the ability to see beyond the obvious."

Before I could interrupt, Holmes continued, "I believe that the way to be a true Christian, Hindu or Muslim is to be true to your religion, while assimilating ideas from other religions. I consider myself to be a true Christian because I have learnt from Hinduism. Similarly, I think of

Singaperumal as a true Hindu because he has learnt elements of Christianity that he says have made him a better Hindu."

"One of the books I have read is the Srimad Bhagavatam. In this book, in 7.5.3, it is said that the great child devotee Prahlada disliked the concept of politics because political philosophy involves considering someone a friend and someone else an enemy. Prahlada saw God in everybody and everything and so did not want to consider anybody as his enemy."

"Similarly, Watson, I try to ensure that I do not treat anybody as an enemy. I have not become an enemy of the Crown by this act. I have merely returned to Lord Ranganatha what is His, that is all."

Mr Singaperumal added, "Dr Watson, one of the things that Mr Holmes has learnt from his study of other religions is the ability to respect the views of others without necessarily subscribing to them. For example, we believe that the Bujagotamma diamond represents Adi Sesha, which translates to the first servant. Adi Sesha thinks of Himself as the first servant of Vishnu. It is a belief among our people that if Adi Sesha is forced to associate with any body else, He will be furious and this will result in great calamity. I don't know if your friend Mr Holmes subscribes to this belief, but he has respected this belief of ours and has returned the diamond to us, for which we are eternally grateful."

"But what use is it to you, Mr Singaperumal? You cannot adore your Lord Ranganatha with it. If you do so, the British will find out and take it away from you."

Before Mr Singaperumal could answer, Holmes said, "The diamond will be hidden in India for the time being, Watson. One of these days, the sun will set over the British Empire in India. When the British rule in India ends, I'm sure that the Bujagotamma diamond can be officially returned to Lord Ranganatha, the rightful owner."

***

Originally appeared in June 2012 on sherlock-holmes.com

Do we need a "new age" Sherlock Holmes?

Should we reinvent The Great Detective so that youngsters can understand him better? Or should we leave this grand icon of a bygone era alone so that we always have a magical world in the past to slip into whenever we need to?

My nephew is today over six years old, and I remember that even when he was just over a year old, he used to say the name of The Great Detective much to my delight. He would say 'cheok omch' when I pointed to a photo of Holmes in my room and since I have written a small book on Holmes*, I hope one day that my nephew will follow in my footsteps and also write about Holmes. But what Holmes will he write about? We know that Sherlock was born on January 6, 1854, and by that reckoning, he is around 155 years old today. If somebody were to write about Holmes when he is 200 years old—and I for one believe that Holmes will be written about even when he turns a thousand—then what stories will one write about?

There are two schools of thought possible here. Those who belong to the old school—and I count myself among such people—will say that Holmes should always be a Victorian character. His world should always be 1895. Any story, written even in 2154 when Holmes is 300 years old should conform to the Victorian period, period. "Here, though the world explode, these two survive, and it is always eighteen ninety-five," as Vincent Starrett wrote.

But there will always be the "modernists" who will say that Holmes should move with the times. They will want us to rewrite (God forbid!) the Canon and have Holmes send an SMS (instead of a telegram) to Watson when he requires the good doctor's help. Should we do this?

Before we answer this question we should engage in a little self-evaluation—what does Holmes represent to each of us? What does he stand for? To some, Holmes is merely a master logician, a brain without a body, a soul without a heart. To many others—and again I wish to be counted among these numbers—he is a friend, somebody who helps us to navigate this modern world with his logic that is unchanging and unchangeable, somebody whose relevance is as much in evidence today as it was yesterday.

Whenever the cares of the modern rat race get to us, we can always slip into 221 B, Baker Street, and listen to the famous Stradivarius, see the 'VR' created by the bullet marks on the wall, view the famous Persian slipper and gaze upon the unanswered correspondence transfixed with a jack-knife to the centre of his wooden mantelpiece. Of course, you can only do this in your mind's eye, but the fact that you can do this means that you can return to the modern world knowing that its abilities to trap you are limited. "The modern rat race can't keep me in a cage," as William P. Schweickert so rightly observed. And for this reason alone we need to ensure that Holmes stays forever in 1895. Not just because he belongs to that age but because a part of each of us too belongs to that era with him.

Originally appeared in May 2009 on sherlock-holmes.com

Happy Birthday Mr Sherlock Holmes!

By Balaji Narasimhan

Every time January 6th comes along, one wishes to remember The Great Detective by celebrating his birthday. But what is the best way of doing this?

One nice way could be reading some of his great stories, but this is something that can be done any other day of the year in the privacy of one's home. We could also smoke a pipe in his honour, but this again is something that is increasingly frowned upon in today's health-conscious world.

So, to truly celebrate, we should perhaps down a peg or two—just small ones, mind you, you do not want The Great Detective to be upset with you turning out to be a drunkard, would you? But if you were to take a small one, you can be sure he wouldn't mind. And even doctors tell us this is good for the heart.

Now that we have decided to have a drink (merely a thimbleful, you understand, and that too just to keep the edge) we should look at what he would approve of. Now, we all know that liquor has played a part in deduction—one remembers the rum from BLAC and the three wine glasses in ABBE—but what did Holmes himself consume?

Even in today's modern world, with its computers that can search for anything, this is not an easy task. Hunting for words like gin and rum through the Canon is made difficult by the fact that these words are used in other contexts—they are a part of words like begin and rummaged—but with the other spirits, it is much easier.

In BLUE, Holmes "ordered two glasses of beer from the ruddy-faced, whiteaproned landlord" while in SCAN too he drinks beer. And before you assume that this is his favourite, turn to SIGN, where he says that he knows his white wines. He has a taste for rare wines too and in LAST, we have seen him sipping I mperial Tokay that comes "from Franz Josef's special cellar at the Schoenbrunn Palace."

Holmes doesn't just drink; he is also a gracious host and offers it to others. The Tokay mentioned above he gladly shared with his good friend Watson— and had Von Bork not been trussed up like chicken on the sofa, we can be sure that Holmes would have offered this to him too.

This is not to suggest that Holmes doesn't show kindness to criminals. In matters of alcohol, he is good to both the good guys and the bad ones, something that we have witnessed in SIGN, when he offers whisky to both Athelney Jones and Jonathan Small. Regarding the latter, Watson writes, "He stopped and held out his manacled hands for the whisky and water which Holmes had brewed for him." In STUD, he offers this drink to Gregson, and in both NOBL and REDH, he partakes of it himself.

All this is fine, you will say, but what is the drink that he would offer you if you were to step into his home on January 6th in order to wish him a happy birthday? In all probability, it would be brandy. While he has been known to partake of this himself in REIG, this seems to be the drink that he offers to most people—examples include Huxtable (PRIO), Eccles (WIST), Ryder (BLUE), Murdoch (EMPT) Phelps (NAVA) and Watson himself (EMPT).

There is a reason for this—most people come to Holmes when they are distraught, and brandy is the best drink for such people under the circumstances. So, even if you ask for Imperial Tokay—and Holmes, being the kind-hearted host, will give it to you—don't be surprised if, in the middle of the birthday revelry, somebody staggers in and faints like Huxtable and is helped to his feet by Holmes with a dash of brandy.

And since this is the drink that Holmes himself keeps handy, maybe this is the right one for us Sherlockians too (just a drop to keep the chill away on his birthday).

Writing this piece has made me thirsty. Could somebody out there hand me a VSOP, please?

***

Sherlock's Illusion

Here's a puzzle based on the Beale ciphers—with an interesting twist.

Read the letter to Sherlock Holmes and the letter from Sherlock Holmes and see if you can find the murderer.

The Letter to Sherlock Holmes

Dear Mr. Sherlock Holmes,

Recently, the wife of a prominent High Official was found murdered in her house.

It has been established beyond all doubt that, at the time of the murder, there were only two other people in the house—the High Official himself, and the guard, Barani.

The Director General has assigned me the case, and I am keen on solving it because my promotion depends on this.

Additionally, I also hold the deceased in great esteem because she worked tirelessly to uproot corruption. This is ironic because her husband the High Official is himself said to be corrupt. Naturally, this had led to some amount of friction between the couple. However, I don't believe that the High Official had anything to do with the murder.

Warm Regards,

Inspector Srinivasan Singaperumal
New Delhi

The Letter from Sherlock Holmes

Dear Mr. Srinivasan Singaperumal,

Thank you for your kind note. At present, I am quite busy, so I don't think that I can be of any assistance.

I'm currently analyzing a puzzle that appeared in *La Revue des Jeux* on 21st August 1891. Here is the partially completed puzzle:

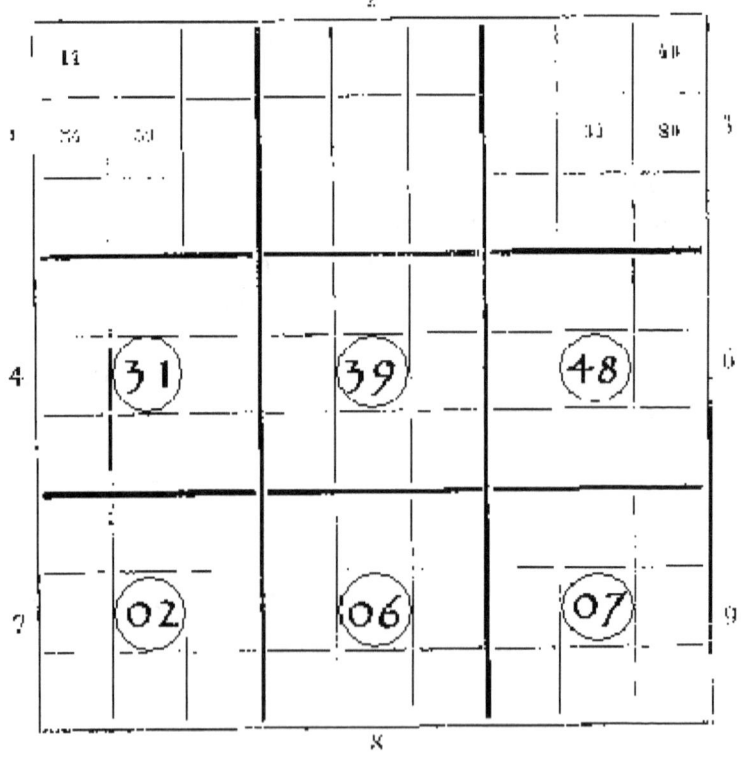

I have circled the figures that I have added. I hope that you are able to solve both the murder and the puzzle. If I may quote myself from The Adventure of the Musgrave Ritual, "It may be that the solution of the one may prove to be the solution of the other."

I need to get back to my important work. So, I shall take your leave with a quote by the great Albert Einstein:

RAFFINIERT IS DER HERR GOTT, ABER BOSHAFT IST ER NICHT

I urge you to pray to God, who is subtle, but not malicious.

Warm Regards,

Sherlock Holmes
South Downs

The Explanation

If you know how the Beale ciphers work, you will do the following:

Number	Character	Number	Character	Number	Character
1	R	19	H	37	S
2	A	20	E	38	H
3	F	21	R	39	A
4	F	22	R	40	F
5	I	23	<SPACE>	41	T
6	N	24	G	42	<SPACE>
7	I	25	O	43	I
8	E	26	T	44	S
9	R	27	T	45	T
10	T	28	,	46	<SPACE>
11	<SPACE>	29	<SPACE>	47	E
12	I	30	A	48	R
13	S	31	B	49	<SPACE>
14	<SPACE>	32	E	50	N
15	D	33	R	51	I
16	E	34	<SPACE>	52	C
17	R	35	B	53	H
18	<SPACE>	36	O	54	T

Putting together the characters pertaining to the circled figures, you will get **BARANI**.

So, you will feel that Holmes feels that Barani is the killer.

80

And yet, Srinivasan Singaperumal arrested the High Official because he saw through the illusion meant for the High Official, whom Holmes suspected would try to use his powerful office to intercept the communication he had sent to Srinivasan Singaperumal and evade the law.

Srinivasan Singaperumal realized that Holmes could have just said "Barani." The fact that he used an elaborate plot made him realize that Barani was not the killer—after all, why should Holmes go through all this for a guard?

* * *

Sherlock Holmes and The Nakshatras Of Vesuvius

DEDICATION

This petite work is dedicated to two petite people—
my dear adorably mischievous nephew Pranav, who
erupts like Vesuvius, and my best gold standard
pal Juliana, who doesn't.

TABLE OF CONTENTS

AUTHOR'S NOTE

SHERLOCK HOLMES HAS A VISITOR

SHERLOCK HOLMES SENDS A TELEGRAM

SHERLOCK HOLMES DESCRIBES INDIAN
ASTROLOGY

SHERLOCK HOLMES ON THE SARVATO BHADRA
CHAKRA

SHERLOCK HOLMES 'MARCH'ES ON

AUTHOR'S NOTE

Come to think about it, there is a lot in common between the detective and the astrologer.

Both need to consider issues from various angles. Both need to analyze data thoroughly before arriving at a conclusion. Both need to consider various factors that could have a bearing upon the case. Both need to eliminate factors that do not have a chance of fructification in order to arrive at the truth. And finally, both need to rely extensively upon logic, reasoning and deduction.

Since I happen to be a fan of Sherlock Holmes and also have a keen interest in Jyotish, I felt that this would be an ideal way of approaching the matter. Also, instead of just tossing 20 charts at people and analyzing them in a dry fashion, I felt that this could make things both lively and educative at the same time.

Please note that, while this is in some ways a work of the imagination, a lot of details presented here are facts. The dates of the 20 eruptions of Vesuvius are real, and have been taken from www.vesuvioinrete.it. The positions of the grahas relating to March 1944 are also real, and were generated with the DOS tool *SWETEST*, an excellent utility that was downloaded from www.astro.com. The astrological calculations pertaining to the positions of the grahas and their relationships with the nakshatras are also facts, and were calculated by the DOS program *PCJYOTISH*.

This may sound clichéd, but I hope that you enjoy reading this as much as I liked writing it.

Balaji Narasimhan
Bangalore
March 2006

SHERLOCK HOLMES HAS A VISITOR

On 6 Jan 1944, I celebrated my 90th birthday.

A few days later, an old man burst into my humble cottage upon the South Downs without even bothering to knock.

"Mr. Holmes! You must help me!" he said.

I pointed him to a chair and asked, "You have come to consult me about the eruption of Vesuvius, right, Councilman?"

My visitor was at once shocked and impressed. "You are right, Mr. Holmes! Pray tell me, how did you deduce it?"

I leaned back in my chair. "Surely, my deduction is simplicity itself. You speak with an Italian accent, and I know from the papers that Vesuvius erupted on 6 Jan 1944. Since World War II is raging, I knew that as an Italian, you would not have been permitted to make a casual, courtesy call. But still, you managed to enter this country, and this proves that you have power and influence. What could you be, save a Councilman or somebody important in one of the villages surrounding Vesuvius?"

"Amazing!"

"No, elementary," I said. "By the way, I'm sure that you have also had military training, especially with reference to espionage. How else can one explain your ability to come into this country while the war is raging, and you are on the other side? Again, you have come to consult me, so that I can try and save your people, if possible. Again, does not this fact too prove that you are a man holding a prominent position in your town? If you had to just think about yourself, I'm sure that you would have left your village by yourself. Am I not right?"

"Excellent, Mr. Holmes! You are completely correct. I can see that, even at this advanced age, your faculties are as sharp as ever. I only pray that you can help me out with my problem. Can you, with your remarkable powers, tell me when Vesuvius will explode?"

I closed the big fat book I was reading, and dropped it on the floor. My age was making me clumsy.

The Italian bent down and picked it up for me. Glancing upon the characters on the cover, he asked, "What is this book, Mr. Holmes?"

"It is an ancient Sanskrit book called 'Hora Shastra,' which was written several thousands of years ago by an Indian sage called Parasara. A good Indian friend gifted it to me a few decades ago. It is a really fascinating book, and if you knew Sanskrit, I would have urged you to read it too."

"Ah, well, quite interesting, I suppose, in its own way, whatever it is. However, Mr. Holmes, I beg that you stop reading this book for the time being and

87

concentrate upon my problem. If Vesuvius explodes anytime soon, all my people are doomed!"

"Actually," I said, "This book could hold the key to your problem."

"I'm surprised, Mr. Holmes. What could an Indian sage, who lived thousands of years ago, have to do with Vesuvius erupting?"

"This question I shall answer in good time. By the way, in order to help me, can you give me some dates when Vesuvius exploded? As many as you can, please—it will, I feel, greatly enhance the accuracy of my research if you could."

"That's easy, Mr. Holmes!" said the Italian. "Every man in my village knows these details by heart."

The Italian then took pen and paper and wrote down the following:

#	DATE
A	16 DEC 1631
B	03 JUL 1660
C	13 APR 1694
D	25 MAY 1698
E	28 JUL 1707
F	20 MAY 1737
G	23 DEC 1760
H	19 OCT 1767
I	08 AUG 1779
J	15 JUN 1794
K	22 OCT 1822
L	23 AUG 1834
M	06 FEB 1850
N	01 MAY 1855
O	08 DEC 1861
P	15 NOV 1868
Q	24 APR 1872
R	04 APR 1906
S	03 JUN 1929

"Here's my card, Mr. Holmes," he said after finishing. "I appeal to you, please don't mention my name to anybody, or I could suffer because we are on opposite sides in this War."

"Do not worry," I said. "But, be ready to act. I will send you a telegram if I get anything concrete."

"Goodbye, Mr. Holmes."   "Goodbye."

SHERLOCK HOLMES SENDS A TELEGRAM

After my Italian visitor left—I shall refrain from mentioning his name since I have given him my word—I sat down and worked feverishly. Because of my advanced age, progress was slow, but what I had lost in terms of energy I had gained in terms of patience. Finally, I finished my research, and sent my Italian visitor the following telegram:

VESUVIUS MAY ERUPT ON 18 MARCH 1944

The event mentioned above happened as I had anticipated it. Thanks to my telegram, the people in the village from which my Italian visitor hailed from were saved.

I got a hurriedly scribbled thank you note from my Italian friend a few days later, in which he promised to come and visit me later, once things settled down, so that he could thank me personally.

A few months later, my Italian friend came back as promised.

"Mr. Holmes! Thank you very much for saving my people! But, I must know one thing—how did you predict when Vesuvius would explode?"

"As I said, the key was in the Sanskrit book 'Hora Shastra,' which I was reading when we last met. Do you want to know more about it?"

My visitor nodded. And so I began.

SHERLOCK HOLMES DESCRIBES INDIAN ASTROLOGY

"First of all," I told my Italian visitor, "permit me to give you a brief introduction to Indian astrology, which is also called 'Jyotish'."

"Like us Westerners, the Indians also use 12 houses, though they call these same houses by different names:"

HOUSES	WESTERN NAME
MESHA	ARIES
VRISHABA	TAURUS
MITHUNA	GEMINI
KARKATA	CANCER
SIMHA	LEO
KANYA	VIRGO
TULA	LIBRA
VRISCHIKA	SCORPIO
DHANUS	SAGITTARIUS
MAKARA	CAPRICORN
KUMBHA	AQUARIUS
MEENA	PISCES

"The Indians refer to the planets as 'grahas' and this is the list of grahas they use:"

GRAHAS	CODE	WESTERN NAME
SURYA	SU	SUN
CHANDRA	CH	MOON
BUDHA	BU	MERCURY
SUKRA	SK	VENUS
KUJA	KU	MARS
GURU	GU	JUPITER
SANI	SA	SATURN
RAHU	RA	DRAGON'S HEAD
KETU	KE	DRAGON'S TAIL

"But, apart from the grahas, the place where Jyotish is perhaps unique is in the way heavy stress is laid on the stars or the 'nakshatras'. On the next page there is a list of the stars they use:

NAKSHATRA	CODE
ASWINI	ASWI
BHARANI	BHAR
KRITTIKA	KRIT
ROHINI	ROHI
MRIGASHIRSA	MRIG
ARIDRA	ARID
PURNARVASU	PURN
PUSHYA	PUSH
ASLESHA	ASLE
MAKHA	MAKH
POORVA PHALGUNI	PPHA
UTTARA PHALGUNI	UPHA
HASTA	HAST
CHITRA	CHIT
SWATI	SWAT
VISHAKHA	VISH
ANURADHA	ANUR
JEYSHTA	JEYS
MOOLA	MOOL
POORVA SHADA	PASH
UTTARA SHADA	UASH
ABHIJIT	**ABHI**
SRAVANA	SRAV
DHANISHTHA	DHAN
SATABISHA	SATA
POORVA BHADRAPADA	PBHA
UTTARA BHADRAPADA	UBHA
REVATI	REVA

"The list of nakshatras add up to 28. However, the highlighted nakshatra 'abhijit' is usually not used, leaving us with 27 nakshatras."

"All this is very interesting, Mr. Holmes," said my Italian visitor. "But, tell me one thing—which do the Indians consider more important, the houses or the nakshatras?"

"Actually," I told him, "the Indians hold both to be of great importance in prediction. The Indians have divided the 27 nakshatras into quarters called 'padas'. So, we have a total of 27 x 4 = 108 nakshatra padas, which are distributed in the 12 houses at the rate of nine padas per house. Therefore, mesha is said to consist of the four padas of aswi, the four padas of bhar, and the first pada of krit. This order continues, and finally we reach meena, the last house of the zodiac, which consists of the fourth pada of pbha, the four padas of ubha and the four padas of reva. In fact, since the Indians consider the nakshatras to be 'heaped' in the houses, they also call the houses as 'rasi,' which means a heap."

"But," I continued, "We need not bother about all these details. To analyze the eruptions of Vesuvius, all we need to consider are the 27 nakshatras and the 9 grahas."

My visitor rubbed his hands in glee. I was sure that he was not understanding everything—even I had to spend several years in study before I could gain a better understanding of Jyotish—but I could see that he was catching on, and getting more and more interested.

"Now that we have understood about grahas and nakshatras, it is important for us to compute the positions of the grahas on the relevant days. Just as we Westerners say 'the Sun is in Aries on this date,' we have to compute as per the Indian system and come to a conclusion like 'Surya is in Aswini' on this day. For this, we have to use the Indian sidereal zodiac as opposed to the Western tropical zodiac. The Indian sidereal system relies on things like the precession of the equinox and the 'ayanamsa,' which refers to the part of solstice, which needs to be deducted from the positions of the grahas once observations are made by the traditional Western tropical system."

"I will not bother you with the complicated calculations involved. Suffice it to say that, once I had calculated the positions, this is what I got:"

#	SU	CH	BU	SK	KU	GU	SA	RA	KE
A	MOOL	UPHA	JEYS	JEYS	MAKH	REVA	ANUR	BHAR	VISH
B	PURN	KRIT	ARID	MAKH	MAKH	PPHA	SWAT	SWAT	ASWI
C	ASWI	JEYS	BHAR	ASWI	PUSH	PURN	PASH	PASH	ARID
D	ROHI	JEYS	ARID	MRIG	UPHA	VISH	DHAN	CHIT	ASWI
E	PUSH	PUSH	MAKH	ARID	PPHA	PPHA	MRIG	ASWI	CHIT
F	KRIT	DHAN	MRIG	ARID	PURN	PBHA	ROHI	PPHA	PBHA
G	MOOL	PURN	MOOL	SRAV	SRAV	DHAN	PBHA	ROHI	JEYS
H	CHIT	PPHA	SWAT	SWAT	HAST	HAST	ARID	UASH	PUSH
I	ASLE	MRIG	PPHA	PUSH	ANUR	UPHA	VISH	ROHI	JEYS
J	MRIG	PASH	ARID	PURN	CHIT	MOOL	KRIT	ASLE	DHAN
K	SWAT	PASH	VISH	HAST	ANUR	ROHI	BHAR	SRAV	ASLE
L	MAKH	REVA	ASLE	HAST	MRIG	ROHI	HAST	MRIG	MOOL
M	DHAN	JEYS	DHAN	SRAV	MRIG	UPHA	UBHA	MAKH	DHAN
N	BHAR	SWAT	ASWI	ROHI	BHAR	SATA	ROHI	BHAR	VISH
O	JEYS	SATA	ANUR	SRAV	SWAT	UPHA	UPHA	MOOL	ARID
P	VISH	ANUR	SWAT	HAST	MAKH	UBHA	ANUR	ASLE	DHAN
Q	ASWI	VISH	ASWI	REVA	BHAR	PURN	UASH	ROHI	JEYS
R	REVA	PUSH	REVA	ASWI	BHAR	ROHI	SATA	ASLE	DHAN
S	ROHI	REVA	MRIG	ASWI	ASLE	KRIT	MOOL	KRIT	VISH

My visitor glanced at the above table in awe.

"This is quite complicated, Mr. Holmes. How did you analyze all this data and deduce when Vesuvius would erupt next?"

I leaned back in my chair and continued.

"For this, I had to determine what was crucial and what was not. As you have correctly understood, understanding every facet is not necessary. We need not consider all the nine grahas and all the 27 nakshatras."

"We can eliminate what the Indians call the 'natural benefics,' namely Chandra, Budha, Sukra, and Guru. Of course, Chandra and Budha can turn malefic under some circumstances, but we can ignore this because it doesn't have any bearing upon this case. It would be more profitable for us to consider the natural malefics—Surya, Kuja, Sani, Rahu, and Ketu."

"That line of reasoning seems quite logical, Mr. Holmes," said the Italian. "Now, have you arrived at a similar logic for the nakshatras also?"

"I have. Among the 27 nakshatras, some are more worthy of consideration than the others."

"The most important ones are as follows:"

NAKSHATRA	COMMENTS
JANMA NAKSHTRA (01)	THE STAR OF BIRTH
KARMA NAKSHATRA (10)	THE STAR OF WORK
SANGHATIC NAKSHTRA (16)	THE STAR OF COOPERATION
UDAY NAKSHTRA (18)	THE STAR THAT GOVERNS RISE
AADHAN NAKSHTRA (19)	CONSIDERED AS IMPORTANT AS JANMA NAKSHTRA
VINASH NAKSHTRA (23)	THE STAR OF DESTRUCTION
MANAS NAKSHTRA (25)	THE STAR THAT GOVERNS THE MIND
RAJ NAKSHTRA (26)	THE STAR OF ACHIEVEMENT
ABHISHEK NAKSHTRA (27)	ENJOYING THE FRUITS OF ACHIEVEMENT

"Among the 27 nakshatras, these have been considered to be the most important. So, we shall rely on them alone," I explained.

"Amazing, Mr. Holmes! Your logic is indeed fabulous! Now, once you came to these conclusions, what did you do next?"

"Next, my friend, came the hardest point. As you can see from the above chart, all the nakshatras depend upon the position of the first nakshatra you choose. In India, they use the nakshatra in which Chandra is present in order to determine the Janma Nakshatra. For the 19 dates you gave me, I could have studied the charts from this point of view. However, I decided that it would be better to have one fixed nakshatra, from which I would generate my analytical data. After much study, I decided to study all the charts from dhan."

"But why this star, Mr. Holmes? What does it possess, which no other star can be said to have?"

"In the Indian system, Kuja represents fire, and volcano eruptions involve a lot of fire. Also, from aswi, the first nakshatra, dhan becomes the 23rd star, which makes it the natural Vinash Nakshatra or the star of destruction. Also, Kuja is said to 'own' dhan, and is also exalted here. Therefore, I decided, quite firmly, that all my calculations should be based on the consideration that dhan is the Janma Nakshatra for all the 19 eruption days you gave me."

SHERLOCK HOLMES ON THE SARVATO BHADRA CHAKRA

"And then," I continued, "I plotted all the positions of the grahas in the nakshatras using the Sarvato Bhadra Chakra."

"Sarvato Bhadra Chakra? What is that, Mr. Holmes?" asked the visitor.

I showed him the following illustration:

	01							
EE	DHAN	SATA	PBHA	UBHA	REVA	ASWI	BHAR	A
27								
SRAV	RI	G	S	D	CH	L	U	KRIT
ABHI	KH	AI	KUMB	MEEN	MESH	LU	A	ROHI
26								10
UASH	J	MAKR	AH	4, 9, 14 FRI	O	VRIS	V	MRIG
25								
PASH	BH	DHAN	3, 8, 13 THU	5, 10, 15 SAT	1, 6, 11 SUN, TUE	MITH	K	ARID
MOOL	Y	VRIC	AM	2, 7, 12 MON, WED	AU	KATA	H	PURN
23								
JEYS	N	E	TULA	KANY	SIMH	LUU	D	PUSH
ANUR	RI	T	R	P	TH	M	UU	ASLE
		19	18		16			
I	VISH	SWAT	CHIT	HAST	UPHA	PPHA	MAKH	AA

"In the Sarvato Bhadra Chakra, we have to consider what are called 'aspects'. For example, a graha in krit will aspect vish, srav, and bhar. So, in other words, a graha in krit will affect the Abishek Nakshatra (27)."

"Using this logic, I then computed the details of the aspects of the malefic grahas on the nine important nakshatras. This is what my analysis revealed:"

#	01	10	16	18	19	23	25	26	27
A	x				x				x
B			x			x			x
C			x	x		x	x		
D	x	x	x		x	x		x	x
E		x	x		x	x		x	
F			x		x			x	x
G	x				x	x		x	x
H		x	x	x	x	x	x	x	
I	x				x				
J	x	x			x			x	x
K	x				x				x
L		x		x	x		x	x	x
M	x	x		x	x		x	x	x
N	x								
O				x	x	x	x	x	
P	x								x
Q		x	x			x		x	
R	x	x							x
S	x				x				x

"If there is a '×' in a column, it means that that particular nakshatra is affected. For instance, when

Vesuvius erupted on 16 Dec 1631, the Janma Nakshatra was afflicted by one of the five natural malefics. Note that, here, we need not worry about which graha caused the affliction—it is sufficient for us to realize that this specific nakshatra is afflicted."

"This sounds logical, Mr. Holmes. Now, once you had come this far, what did you do next?"

SHERLOCK HOLMES 'MARCH'ES ON

"After coming this far," I continued," I had some reasonable idea about some of the factors that might indicate the next eruption of Vesuvius. Now, the important issue for me to consider was this— would Vesuvius erupt in March 1944? To answer this question, I had to compute the planetary positions of all the nine grahas for March 1944. This is what I got:

DT	SU	CH	BU	SK	KU	GU	SA	RA	KE
01.	SATA	KRIT	DHAN	SRAV	MRIG	ASLE	MRIG	PUSH	SRAV
02.	SATA	ROHI	DHAN	SRAV	MRIG	ASLE	MRIG	PUSH	SRAV
03.	SATA	MRIG	SATA	SRAV	MRIG	ASLE	MRIG	PUSH	SRAV
04.	PBHA	ARID	SATA	SRAV	MRIG	ASLE	MRIG	PUSH	SRAV
05.	PBHA	PURN	SATA	SRAV	MRIG	ASLE	MRIG	PUSH	SRAV
06.	PBHA	PUSH	SATA	SRAV	MRIG	ASLE	MRIG	PUSH	SRAV
07.	PBHA	ASLE	SATA	DHAN	MRIG	ASLE	MRIG	PUSH	SRAV
08.	PBHA	MAKH	SATA	DHAN	MRIG	ASLE	MRIG	PUSH	SRAV
09.	PBHA	PPHA	SATA	DHAN	MRIG	ASLE	MRIG	PUSH	SRAV
10.	PBHA	PPHA	SATA	DHAN	MRIG	ASLE	MRIG	PUSH	SRAV
11.	PBHA	UPHA	PBHA	DHAN	MRIG	ASLE	MRIG	PUSH	SRAV
12.	PBHA	HAST	PBHA	DHAN	MRIG	ASLE	MRIG	PUSH	SRAV
13.	PBHA	CHIT	PBHA	DHAN	MRIG	ASLE	MRIG	PUSH	SRAV
14.	PBHA	SWAT	PBHA	DHAN	MRIG	ASLE	MRIG	PUSH	SRAV
15.	PBHA	VISH	PBHA	DHAN	MRIG	ASLE	MRIG	PUSH	SRAV
16.	PBHA	ANUR	PBHA	DHAN	MRIG	ASLE	MRIG	PUSH	SRAV
17.	PBHA	JEYS	PBHA	SATA	MRIG	ASLE	MRIG	PUSH	SRAV
18.	UBHA	MOOL	UBHA	SATA	MRIG	ASLE	MRIG	PUSH	SRAV
19.	UBHA	PASH	UBHA	SATA	MRIG	ASLE	MRIG	PUSH	SRAV
20.	UBHA	UASH	UBHA	SATA	MRIG	ASLE	MRIG	PUSH	SRAV
21.	UBHA	SRAV	UBHA	SATA	MRIG	ASLE	MRIG	PUSH	SRAV
22.	UBHA	DHAN	UBHA	SATA	MRIG	ASLE	MRIG	PUSH	SRAV
23.	UBHA	SATA	UBHA	SATA	MRIG	ASLE	MRIG	PUSH	SRAV
24.	UBHA	UBHA	UBHA	SATA	MRIG	ASLE	MRIG	PUSH	SRAV
25.	UBHA	REVA	REVA	SATA	MRIG	ASLE	MRIG	PUSH	SRAV
26.	UBHA	ASWI	REVA	SATA	MRIG	ASLE	MRIG	PUSH	SRAV
27.	UBHA	BHAR	REVA	SATA	MRIG	ASLE	MRIG	PUSH	SRAV
28.	UBHA	KRIT	REVA	PBHA	ARID	ASLE	MRIG	PUSH	SRAV
29.	UBHA	ROHI	REVA	PBHA	ARID	ASLE	MRIG	PUSH	SRAV
30.	UBHA	MRIG	REVA	PBHA	ARID	ASLE	MRIG	PUSH	SRAV
31.	REVA	ARID	ASWI	PBHA	ARID	ASLE	MRIG	PUSH	SRAV

"Somehow, I had a gumption that the eruption might be triggered when one of the five malefics changed from one nakshatra to another. Don't ask me how or why I got this feeling—the Indians believe that, while Jyotish is a science with its own set of rules, the intuition of the practitioner is what differentiates a good astrologer from a great one. So, having got this intuition into my head, I decided to test it out.

"Now, you will notice that Sani, Rahu, and Ketu remain in the same star for the whole of March. The only malefic grahas that change stars are Surya, who moves from pbha to ubha on 18th March 1944, and Kuja, who moves from mrig to arid on 28th March 1944."

"This deduction is indeed amazing, Mr. Holmes. Is this when you decided to send me the telegram?"

"No, my friend. I could not risk having you evacuate your village merely because of logic. You see, in Jyotish, it is important that one also test out the logic behind one's reasoning. This is similar to the detective work I used to do in my youth—until something is tested, it cannot be relied upon or trusted."

"Therefore, I decided to take the calculations that I got for 18th March 1944 and then compute them on the Sarvato Bhadra Chakra chart. This is what I got:"

	01			su				
EE	DHAN	SATA	PBHA	UBHA	REVA	ASWI	BHAR	A
27 ke								
SRAV	RI	G	S	D	CH	L	U	KRIT
ABHI	KH	AI	KUMB	MEEN	MESH	LU	A	ROHI
26								10 ku
UASH	J	MAKR	AH	4, 9, 14 FFI	O	VRIS	V	MRIG sa
25								
PASH	BH	DHAN	3, 8, 13 THU	5, 10, 15 SAT	1, 6, 11 SUN, TUE	MITH	K	ARID
MOOL	Y	VRIC	AM	2, 7, 12 MON, WED	AU	KATA	H	PURN
23								rd
JEYS	N	E	TULA	KANY	SIMH	LUU	D	PUSH
ANUR	RI	T	R	P	TH	M	UU	ASLE
			19	18		16		
I	VISH	SWAT	CHIT	HAST	UPHA	PPHA	MAKH	AA

"The chart looks interesting, Mr. Holmes," said my Italian visitor. "But, can you tell me in plain English, please? I could then perhaps understand better."

"Sure," I told him, "In plain English, this is what the chart translates to:"

NAKSHATRA DESCRIPTION	NAKSHATRA NUMBER	NAKSHATRA NAME	AFFECTED BY
JANMA NAKSHTRA	01	DHAN	KETU
KARMA NAKSHTRA	10	MRIG	KUJA, SANI
SANGHATIC NAKSHTRA	16	PPHA	RAHU
UDAY NAKSHTRA	18	HAST	SURYA
AADHAN NAKSHTRA	19	CHIT	KUJA, SANI
VINASHA NAKSHTRA	23	JEYS	RAHU
MANAS NAKSHTRA	25	PASH	SURYA
RAJ NAKSHTRA	26	UASH	KUJA, SANI
ABHISHEK NAKSHTRA	27	SRAV	KETU

"Though you have seen the chart concerning afflictions of the nine critical nakshatras in all the 19 cases, let me again present to you the chart with all the 20 cases, so that you are able to fully appreciate the reason why I was so sure Vesuvius would erupt on 18th March 1944:"

DATE	01	10	16	18	19	23	25	26	27
16 DEC 1631	✗				✗				✗
03 JUL 1660			✗			✗			✗
13 APR 1694			✗	✗		✗	✗		
25 MAY 1698	✗	✗	✗		✗	✗		✗	✗
28 JUL 1707		✗	✗		✗	✗		✗	
20 MAY 1737			✗		✗			✗	✗
23 DEC 1760	✗				✗	✗		✗	✗
19 OCT 1767		✗	✗	✗	✗	✗	✗	✗	
08 AUG 1779	✗					✗			
15 JUN 1794	✗	✗			✗			✗	✗
22 OCT 1822	✗					✗			✗
23 AUG 1834		✗		✗	✗		✗	✗	✗
06 FEB 1850	✗	✗		✗	✗		✗	✗	✗
01 MAY 1855	✗								
08 DEC 1861				✗	✗	✗	✗	✗	
15 NOV 1868	✗								✗
24 APR 1872		✗	✗			✗		✗	
04 APR 1906	✗	✗							✗
03 JUN 1929	✗				✗				✗
18 MAR 1944	✗	✗	✗	✗	✗	✗	✗	✗	✗

"As you can see, on 18th March 1944, all the nine critical nakshatras were afflicted, something that had never happened whenever Vesuvius had exploded earlier."

"This confirmed my view that there was a high probability that Vesuvius would erupt on that day. It was only after I confirmed my suspicions that I decided to inform you in order to take necessary precautions, like evacuating your village."

"And for this help that you have rendered me, Mr. Holmes, both I and all my people will forever be indebted to you. Many thanks, sir! You are indeed a genius!"

"No," I disagreed, "but Parasara most certainly is. Maybe, you need to thank Parasara, and my good Indian friend, Dr. Srinivasan Singaperumal, who gifted me the 'Hora Shastra' by Parasara."

A Study in Regret

www.mxpublishing.com

Also from MX Publishing

Winners of the 2011 Howlett Literary Award (Sherlock
Holmes book of the year) for '**The Norwood Author**'
From the world's largest Sherlock Holmes publisher dozens of
new novels from the top Holmes authors.
www.mxpublishing.com

Including our bestselling short story collections 'Lost Stories of
Sherlock Holmes' , 'The Outstanding Mysteries of Sherlock
Holmes', 'Untold Adventures of Sherlock Holmes' (and the
sequel 'Studies in Legacy) and 'Sherlock Holmes in Pursuit'.